The Day It Rained Hearts

Felicia Bond

LAURA GERINGER BOOKS

An Imprint of HarperCollins*Publishers*

Previously published as *Four Valentines in a Rainstorm*

Library of Congress Cataloging-in-Publication Data
Bond, Felicia.
     The day it rained hearts / Felicia Bond.
          p.   cm.
     Summary: On the day it rains hearts, Cornelia Augusta
makes Valentine cards for four of her friends.
     ISBN-10: 0-06-623876-5 (trade bdg.) — ISBN-13: 978-0-06-623876-0 (trade bdg.)
     ISBN-10: 0-06-001078-9 (lib. bdg.) — ISBN-13: 978-0-06-001078-2 (lib. bdg.)
     ISBN-10: 0-06-073123-0 (pbk.) — ISBN-13: 978-0-06-073123-6 (pbk.)
     [1. Valentine's Day—Fiction.   2. Valentines—Fiction.]
I. Title.
PZ7.B63666Fo 1983   82-45586
[E]   CIP
                                                      AC

❖

Originally published under the title
Four Valentines in a Rainstorm

Especially for Roger

One day it started raining hearts,

and Cornelia Augusta caught one.

She caught another,

and another.

It wasn't very hard, so she caught some more.

"It must be getting close to Valentine's Day," she thought,

and she set to work making Valentines.
The hearts she caught would make
perfect cards.

Cornelia Augusta saw that all of her hearts were different.

She looked at each one

from the front,

and the back,

and the side,

and decided which ones would be just

right for each of her friends.

She found seven that were more or less alike and strung them together with a needle and thread.

"I know just the right person for this one," she thought.

Then Cornelia Augusta took an especially handsome heart and pasted it on a piece of paper.

In the center of the heart she glued a
cotton ball, one that was very white
and very soft. And she knew instantly
who this card would be for.

Cornelia Augusta had eight hearts left.

On the largest one she drew circles and
then very carefully cut them out.

The other hearts were *so* small, she arranged all of them on one piece of paper. Around the hearts she painted patterns of many colors. Then she folded her design in half.

There was no doubt in her mind

who would receive these.

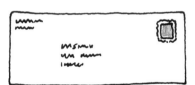

Cornelia Augusta put a stamp on each
of her Valentines

and mailed them.

It never rained hearts again—

not where Cornelia Augusta lived, anyway—

but it didn't matter,

because the next year,

and the next,

and all the years after that,

Cornelia Augusta

found other ways to make Valentines.